The Book of Complements

David Rowinski

Inknbeans Press

Cover by Evonne
Copyright November 2013 David Rowinski and
Inknbeans Press

ISBN-13: 978-0615919898 (Inknbeans Press)
ISBN-10:0615919898

I

A crystal sphere

balanced

upon a

point

attracts the attention

of a passing serpent.

Cautious,

    it approaches,

        forked tongue darting

            to sniff the air.

Curious,

it coils about the orb.

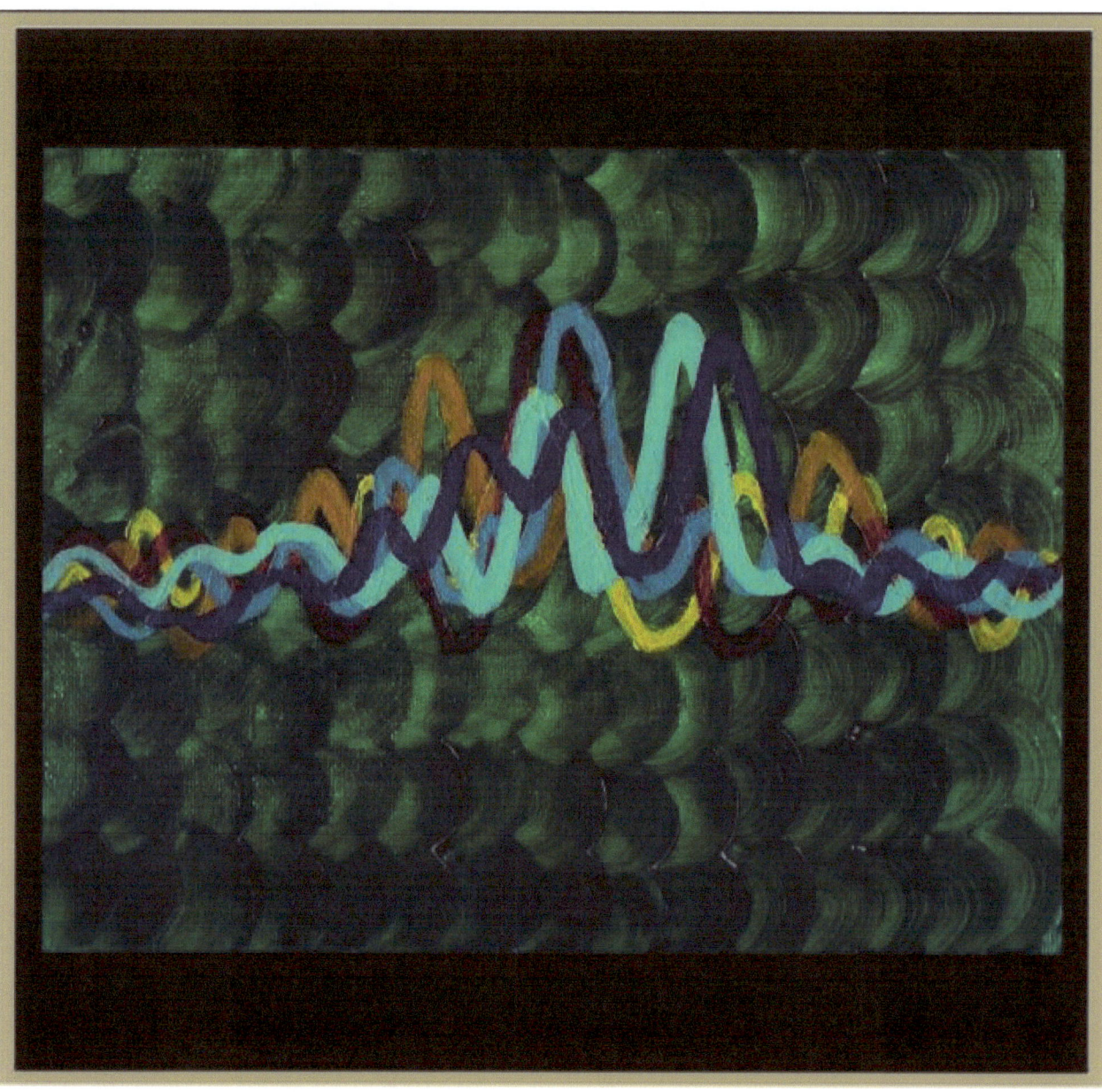

Constricting,
it feels vibrations radiating
from the stone's center

ripple
as song along scaled skin.

Lidless eyes watch,
transfixed by sound
possessing the
sphere's interior.

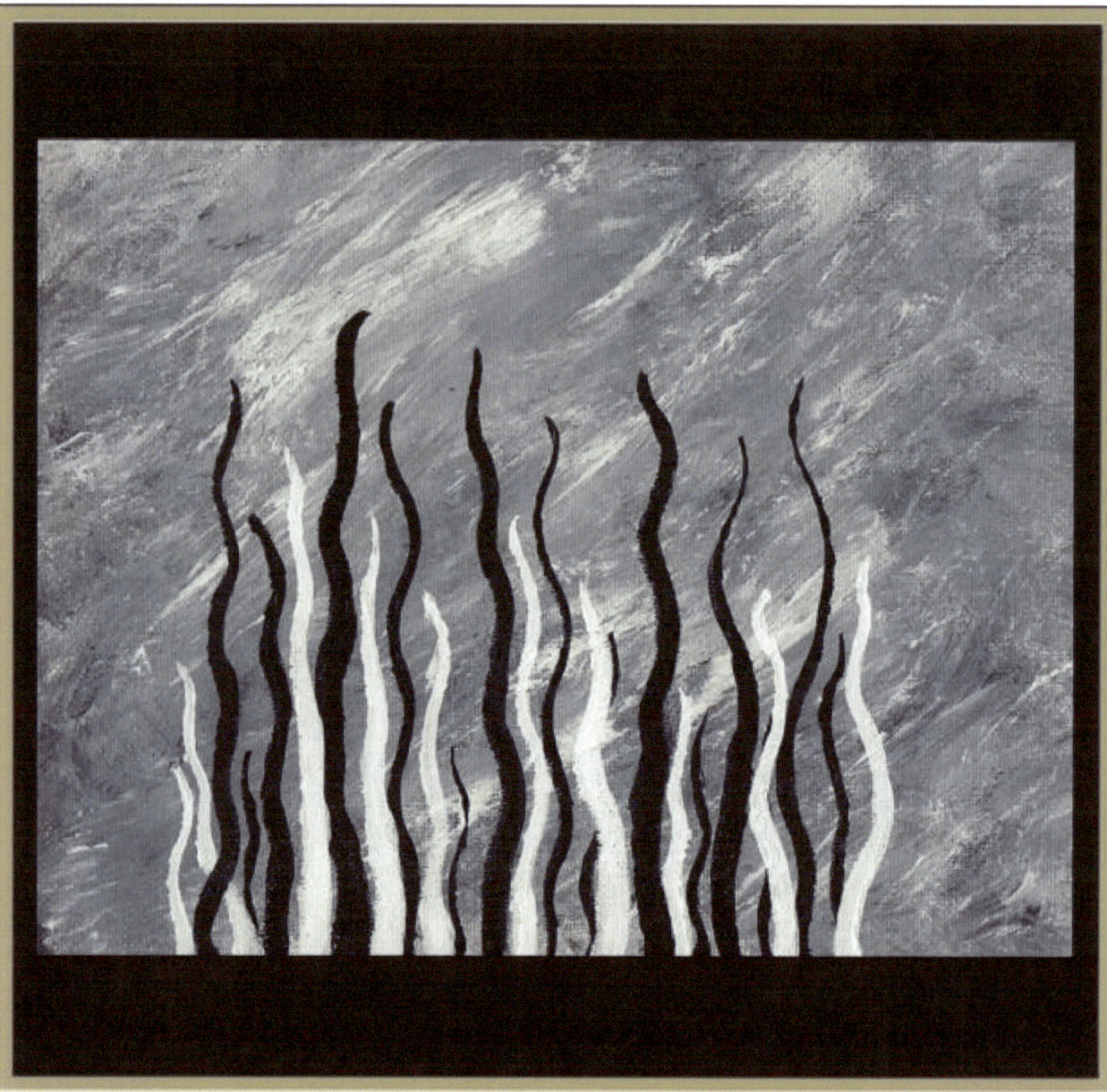

At the poles, strands
of elements gently sway.

Suddenly released,
they drift through
the depths
borne on music

until mutual attraction

generates pairs.

True and False form a corkscrew

Fast loops around Slow

Young twists about Old

Awake winds around Asleep

Long whirls about Short

Light orbits around Dark

Dry twirls about Wet
Up swings around Down
Right spins about Left
Hot weaves around Cold
Beauty wraps about Ugliness
Good and Evil form a helix.

The serpent tastes the possibility of attaining perfection by extracting only the elements it desires.

Approaching True, it whispers,
"Your purity is soiled by False."

Then, seeking to ease
discomfort, it says,
"Light, cast off the shadow
obscuring the glory
of your radiance.
Join Hot and Dry.
Dark, Cold and Wet
should be forgotten."

With further compliments,
it plants seeds of dissent
that take root
with Long, Young and Fast,
Awake, Up and Right.

Falling prey to flattery,
Beauty and Good
lead the elements from
the crystal's confines,
causing space to resound
with a thunderous
rainbow flash.

Guided by True and Good
beyond False and Evil,
the serpent acts solely
on instinct, slithering
away from the broken
sphere driven by a throat
parched by Dry.

Wisdom lost
when Young
abandoned Old,
while stricken
with Beauty,
it cannot recognize Long
drawing its body beyond measure.

Moving Fast and ever Right,
it spirals up,
dizzy, confused,
perpetually Awake.

Blinded by Light
then scorched with Hot,
the serpent is devoured by flame.

II

The glint of shattered crystal
catches the eye of a bird

that drops
from the sky
to land amidst
the devastation of
broken complements.

It scratches and pecks
through shards and ashes
seeking material
to compose a nest.

Exposing the disconnected strands
of elements, it silently picks out
Good and Evil, then takes
flight with a sense of purpose.

Spotting a solitary tree
upon an empty plain,
the bird descends
to set down its burden
before returning to gather
the remaining threads.

True mixes with False

Fast ties with Slow

Young combines with Old

Long unites with Short

Dry blends with Wet

Right fuses with Left
Up melds with Down
Hot mingles with Cold
Beauty joins with Ugliness
Dark connects with Light.

Finally setting
Awake and Asleep
in place,
the bird settles into its nest
closing its eyes to dream.

A crystal sphere

balanced

upon a

point

In Memorium

Joseph J

and

Peggy A

Rowinski

Having travelled the roads of Egypt, Greece, Hungary, and Switzerland, David Rowinski now divides time between Kenya, Tanzania and Massachusetts.

In the Open Pillow he explored the process of growth and exponential thinking to find ones place. The Book of Complements is the first of a planned series of graphic myths.

Profits from the sale of this book will be donated to Leko Arts Organization based in Kenya. Leko is a Luo word meaning 'to dream.' Founded by the East African performer Sali Oyugi, the organization aims to nurture the dreams and develop the talents of children by establishing arts centers in under resourced neighborhoods. Through professional instruction in visual, performing, and multi-media arts, Leko's vision is to see vulnerable youth thrive and turn into responsible citizens.

www.ingramcontent.com/pod-product-compliance
Lightning Source LLC
Chambersburg PA
CBHW041011170626
46815CB00003B/259